young adult
novel

Also by Daniel Pinkwater
Java Jack

young adult novel

by Daniel Pinkwater

THOMAS Y. CROWELL   NEW YORK

Library of Congress Cataloging in Publication Data

Pinkwater, Daniel Manus, 1941–
Young adult novel.
SUMMARY: The Wild Dada Ducks members cause
all sorts of mischief around their junior high school,
but although the boys are not bad,
they like to pretend that they are true dadaists
with unintentional and irrational behavior.
   [1. Dadaism—Fiction. 2. School stories] I. Title.
PZ7.P6335Yp 1982   [Fic]   81-43391
ISBN 0-690-04188-8   AACR2   ISBN 0-690-04189-6 (lib. bdg.)

1 2 3 4 5 6 7 8 9 10
First Edition

To Charles—more than a cat

1

Kevin's new social worker was Mr. Justin Jarvis, and Kevin didn't like him one bit. He was constantly smiling, and he spoke in a smooth, soft, voice that made Kevin nervous.

Most annoying was the knowledge that Kevin depended on Mr. Jarvis completely. Kevin's mother was in the madhouse. Mr. Jarvis called it a psychiatric facility—but it was a madhouse, nothing else—and Kevin's mother was mad. She had gone mad the day Kevin's father had been in the accident at the methane works —the day he had been deprived of speech, sight, and hearing, and the use of his legs. Dad was in the veteran's hospital now, little better than a vegetable.

When Kevin was taken to visit his father, all he could do was sit and stare at the broken form in the wheelchair. His father horrified him, and made him feel angry. "How could you leave me like this?" Kevin thought.

What was Scott Shapiro, Kevin's father, thinking about in the wheelchair? Was he remembering the day he had been blown into darkness and silence forever by the exploding methane tank? Was he remembering that last morning, before the accident, before his wife, Cynthia, had gone mad? Was he remembering the news that had come that morning, that Kevin's sister, Isobel, had been arrested for prostitution?

As far as Kevin knew, Isobel was still downtown, working the bars across the street from the bus station. He wished he could talk to her. Isobel had always been the only one in the Shapiro family who understood Kevin.

Maybe some day Isobel would be brought in to the alcoholism treatment center where Kevin was staying. There was always a chance of that. Kevin had done his earliest drinking with Isobel.

If the vice squad ever caught her, they might bring her to the alcoholism treatment center. She wouldn't be sent to regular jail—after all, she was only fifteen— just two years older than Kevin.

Kevin felt the wad of money in his sock. He had earned sixty-five dollars that morning, selling pills to the other kids in the treatment center. In addition, he had twenty dollars he had stolen from Mr. Jarvis.

So here was Kevin, a thirteen-year-old alcoholic,

pusher, and thief. His mother would probably never get well, his father certainly wouldn't, and sister Isobel was turning tricks on State Street. It seemed to Kevin that there wasn't a chance in the world that he would ever get his life straightened out.

And he was right. So we hit him over the head and fed him to the pigs.

2

This is Charles the Cat speaking. The sad story of Kevin the messed-up thirteen-year-old is one of the pastimes of the Wild Dada Ducks. It is a story entitled, *Kevin Shapiro, Boy Orphan*. The Wild Dada Ducks tell this story to one another. Each Wild Dada Duck makes up as much of the story as he likes, and the story is always changing. Sometimes Kevin is an orphan, sometimes a juvenile delinquent, a druggie, a lonely child of feuding parents, a social misfit, a homosexual, a weakling who wants to play sports, and any number of other kinds of hard-luck characters.

Kevin Shapiro, Boy Orphan is different from the novels in the Himmler High School library in that he never solves his problems. Instead, we usually kill him from time to time. Kevin is indestructible. You can kill him as often as you like. He can be brought back to life in the next chapter, which usually gets told the following day during lunch.

In addition to myself, Charles the Cat, the other Wild Dada Ducks are the Honorable Venustiano Carranza (President of Mexico), Captain Colossal, Igor, and the Indiana Zephyr. Those are not our real names—they are our Dada names. We don't use our real names anymore.

There is also the Duckettes, the Wild Dada Ducks ladies' auxiliary, which has no member at all at present. Should suitable females present themselves for membership in the Duckettes, we will consider them, but there have been no applicants as yet. Dada is generally a misunderstood art movement.

It was the Honorable Venustiano Carranza (President of Mexico) who first told us about Dada. In those days El Presidente was known as Pecos Bill. When we heard about Dada, we all agreed to devote our lives to it, took new names, and began our historically important work of reshaping culture, righting the wrongs of the past, and producing new works of Dada Art. Starting with Himmler High School, we intend to bring about a world Dada Renaissance. We have already written a Wild Dada Duck Manifesto.

THE WILD DADA DUCK MANIFESTO
On this, the natal day of Marcel Duchamp (the first Tuesday of every month at 4:00 PM), the

5

Board of Medical Advisors of the Empire of Japan declares that the institution formerly known as Margaret Himmler High School will henceforth become the Municipal Vacuum Cleaner. Teachers will report for re-processing as diesel railroad locomotives, and students will adopt the appearance and function of electro-computerized kitchen appliances. Those who choose not to comply with the ruling of the Imperial Medical Board will be required to present a paper cup not filled with cherry pits or gravel at the office of the ex-administrator of unexpected nasal events. All others will be required to present paper cups *not* filled with cherry pits or gravel at the nose of the official administrator of ex-events. By this simple measure, world peace, brotherhood, and unlimited happiness has been secured for all mechano-humanoids.

Fellow machines! Dis-unite! This call to arms, torsos, and feet will not be repeated except by request.

One hundred thousand copies of the Wild Dada Duck Manifesto, printed on black paper with black ink were not made, and were not distributed to the students and faculty of Himmler High. This was the first important action of the Wild Dada Ducks, and it was met, as we hoped it would be, with wild indifference.

By the way, it turns out that the Honorable Venustiano Carranza (President of Mexico) had not made

Dada up in his own head. It is a real movement, and Marcel Duchamp was a real person. I found that out only after being a Dadaist myself for months.

3

At this point, I would like to describe the members of the Wild Dada Ducks. The Honorable Venustiano Carranza (President of Mexico) is tall and thin. The Indiana Zephyr is tall and thin. I, Charles the Cat, am not tall, and thin. Captain Colossal is tall and not thin. Igor is not tall and not thin. Because Dada is a serious movement, we try to remain dignified in expression and dress. We laugh as little as possible, at least in the presence of others, and we always wear neckties. My favorite necktie is black with a red plastic fish about five inches long attached to it with miracle glue. The Honorable Venustiano Carranza (President of Mexico) has a wheel from a baby carriage which he wears on a chain around his neck, over his tie. Igor has a banana on a string which he wears around his neck. He talks with the banana, whose name is Freddie, and also uses it as a mock microphone and make-believe pistol. Captain Colossal and the Indiana Zephyr are also stylish, but they do not have one favorite kind of attire—they alter their appearance from day to day.

This brings me to the response to the presence of the Wild Dada Ducks on the part of the other students at Himmler High. I am sorry to say that a great many of them are hostile to our Dadaistic expression of our innermost feelings. I am even sorrier to say that many more of the Himmler students are not hostile. They are totally indifferent. As far as I know, the Wild Dada Ducks have no active supporters in the school—not even any sympathizers. In a nutshell, they don't care about us, or they hate us. This includes teachers.

Of course, being resourceful Dadaists, we have decided to capitalize on the situation as it exists. Our every move as Wild Dada Ducks is calculated to make people ignore or detest us all the more. In this way, the population of Himmler High is doing what we want it to, without knowing it.

Of course we don't take any of the indifference or abuse personally. It is not as individuals that we are hated and ignored, but as Dadaists. What is more, we recognize our responsibility to educate and enlighten the people at Himmler.

And so, we are very busy Wild Dada Ducks. Some examples: In the main hall of Himmler High there is a large glass display case. It has electric lights in it, and

9

was formerly used to display trophies won by the school's teams. Some time ago vandals opened the case and stole the trophies. There was a big uproar about it. As Wild Dada Ducks, we approved of this, feeling that the vandals might be groping their way toward Dadaism—and wrote a letter to the school paper saying so. The letter was never printed. The Wild Dada Ducks discussed this, and decided that the school was unable to deal with our clear-sighted philosophical analysis of the theft because it was grieving over the loss of the trophies. As a humanitarian gesture, we decided to give the school a new trophy, a better one than all the ones that had been stolen.

It was easily done. First we went to a junk-yard and bought a fine used toilet—just the bowl, without the tank or seat. This we lovingly cleaned and polished until it was very beautiful, and looked much better than new. The only difficult part was getting access to the empty display case—but since there was nothing in it, it wasn't particularly closely watched. With a giant pair of pliers, Igor smashed the dinky cheap lock on the case. We then placed the shining, lovely, toilet in the case. (We had smuggled the art object, wrapped in brown paper into the school the day before.) We turned on the electric lights. Then we replaced the dinky cheap lock with a new, beautiful one, made of brass, and very shiny. To prevent future vandals from getting into the case, we left the keys for the lock inside, next to the beautiful toilet. We had polished them too.

The total effect was wonderful! The toilet bowl

gleamed in the warm electric light, and made all the Wild Dada Ducks very proud and happy. Now all the people at Himmler would be able to take pride again. Now there was a trophy even finer and more significant in place of the cheap ordinary ones that had been stolen. What was more, now all the people at Himmler would have a chance to think about what a beautiful object a toilet is! We had done a heroic thing.

And was it appreciated? Of course not! There were only two opinions expressed by all who saw our work of art. Some thought it was terrible, and some thought it was funny. However, everybody came to see it, and nothing else was talked about for the two days the toilet remained in the case, shining like a beacon of truth in the main hall of Himmler High.

The principal had our magnificently polished lock removed with a hacksaw, and the art work was removed and discarded—it would wind up on the same dump we had gotten it from.

Everybody suspected that we were the artists, but we remained silent. After all, we did not do what we did for credit, but for the benefit of mankind.

And now a word about Dada music. The Wild Dada Ducks are happy to note that there's a lot of very acceptable Dada music being performed these days. This is the only area in which the kids at Himmler show any signs of culture. Some of the groups approved by the Wild Dada Ducks are the Slugs, The Yeggs, The Noggs, and The Yobs.

4

Kevin Shapiro, Boy Orphan, Chapter One Thousand Fifteen:

Kevin didn't want anyone to see him thinking about Aunt Lucille, because whenever he thought about her there was a good chance he might cry. It made Kevin feel all soft and weepy when he remembered sitting in front of the huge stone fireplace at Red Oaks, Aunt Lucille's great house in the Kentucky Blue Grass country. There, Kevin had had his own little room up in the attic, and his own Thoroughbred horse to train and ride. Winky was the name of Kevin's horse, and he had fed him and cared for him from the time he was a little colt. It had looked as though Winky had a great future as a racer, and Kevin was going to ride him in the Kentucky Derby.

All that changed the day Kevin was sent to Lexington with Simms, the handyman. They had driven over in Aunt Lucille's Rolls Royce to get a new silver snaffle for Winky. How could Kevin have known that something would go horribly wrong at the nuclear reactor in Cogginsville, just two miles away from Red Oaks? How could Kevin have known that Aunt Lucille and Winky, and all the other horses, and Red Oaks itself would light up with a strange blue glow, and that the entire place would be put off limits, and quarantined forever by the Atomic Energy Commission? Kevin would never see Winky and Aunt Lucille again—and how was he to know? Still, Kevin felt that somehow it was all his fault.

Another artistic project of the Wild Dada Ducks was our play, *Chickens From Uranus,* a science-fiction thriller. We made wonderful posters to announce our play. They had pictures of heavy machinery and really nice angular lettering that Igor does. It's almost illegible.

We put the play on in the lunchroom. Here it is:
CHICKENS FROM URANUS
Adapted from *MacBeth* by William Shakespeare

Dramatis Personae

TICK AND TOCK, *two Roman Emperors*
LORD BUDDHA, *a rock star*
HENRY FORD, *a teen-age starlet*
THE DEVIL, *the devil*

13

(All the characters appear wearing paper bags over their heads. The bags are decorated with cutouts of pictures of bulldozers, tractors, military tanks, automobiles, and chickens.)

TICK:	Moo! Moo! Moo! Moo!
TOCK:	Arf! Arf! Arf! Arf!
BUDDHA:	Woo! Woo! Woo! Woo!
H. FORD:	Meow! Meow! Meow! Meow!
THE DEVIL:	(Whistles like a bird)
ALL:	(Leafing through a deck of cards) Three of clubs. Jack of diamonds. Two of clubs. Ace of diamonds. Five of hearts. Queen of spades. Two of spades. King of clubs . . . (and so on until all the cards have been read).
ALL:	(Hum) Mmmmmmmmmmmmm. Mmmmmmmmmmmm. Mmmmmmmmmmmm.

Finis

It isn't much of a script in terms of length, but the actual performance took a good twenty minutes, because we spoke extremely slowly, and moved very slowly, like robots. It was a great performance, and to prove it, nobody paid any attention to it. The best actor was Captain Colossal, who had the part of Henry Ford. It took him almost half a minute just to say "meow."

Amazingly, we were summoned by the Lord High

Executioner (that's Mr. Gerstenblut, the vice-principal), as a result of our performance. He said that Himmler High School did not approve of our activities. He said that we had disrupted the lunch period by putting on an unauthorized play. Naturally, we thanked him for praising us, at which point he got angry. He shouted at us. He also told us that we were in violation of the Himmler High School Dress Code by wearing fish and baby-carriage wheels around our necks. And lobsters. On this particular day, the Indiana Zephyr was wearing a very large red plastic lobster which we all admired.

Mr. Gerstenblut told us that if we didn't shape up we'd be in trouble.

Even though the Wild Dada Ducks are pacific, peaceful, non-violent, and even ultra-non-violent, we will not run from a fight if there is no other way. It was clear to us that Mr. Gerstenblut was making an ultimatum which could lead to only one response. War.

Kevin Shapiro, Boy Orphan, Chapter Six Thousand Four Hundred and One.

Kevin's head was swimming. Could it be? Was it possible, after only doing it once? Of course, he'd heard of it happening to other kids, but somehow he had never considered it as something that could happen to him. After all, Brenda knew what she was doing —she had told him so. She had said not to worry. Kevin had believed her. He had trusted her. He knew Brenda wouldn't lie, but now, here he was, looking at the doctor's face, which loomed as large as a face on a movie screen. The doctor had a kindly expression, but it all seemed like some kind of horrible nightmare. "Yes, there's no doubt about it," the doctor was saying to Kevin, "you are two months pregnant."

5

The most aggravating thing the Lord High Executioner said to us was that since the Wild Dada Ducks was not an officially sanctioned Himmler High School student activity, as far as he was concerned, the Wild Dada Ducks did not exist.

We held a council of war. It was decided that we could not overlook this insult. Venustiano Carranza (President of Mexico) made a stirring speech. Igor and the Indiana Zephyr wanted to engage in prolonged terrorism, but Captain Colossal reminded them that any action we might take should be in keeping with our Dadaist principles.

There was some discussion of flooding the library

and holding war canoe races there as a gesture of indifference to Mr. Gerstenblut's ill-mannered remark. While everyone agreed that the idea had merit, and it would be worth looking into for some future activity, it was generally felt that our response to Mr. Gerstenblut's insolence should be expressed more directly, even though that would not be the most Dada approach.

Finally, it was decided that, since the Lord High Executioner had questioned our existence, that the appropriate response would be to bring his existence into question.

It was agreed that we would issue a public statement of Mr. Gerstenblut's lack of reality, failure to be, and non-presence, in the world as we know it.

Captain Colossal printed up several hundred cards in the print shop. To make it classier, we printed them in French.

Horace Gerstenblut
n'existe pas.

Since less than 3% of the kids at Himmler take French, there was considerable interest in the cards. People didn't know what they said. Also, we distributed them in an interesting way. We put stacks of them in the bathrooms of both sexes. People picked them up when they went to the bathroom, and handed them around.

Not only did we have revenge on Mr. Gerstenblut, it was also the most successful work of Art so far undertaken by the Wild Dada Ducks. That is, it was the first thing we had done in which people had taken such an active interest. We were a little sorry we hadn't printed something about Dada on the card.

We knew the cards were a big success because Igor takes French, and dozens of people asked him to translate the *Horace Gerstenblut n'existe pas* cards they were carrying around with them.

We didn't know how much of a success the cards were until the last period of the day, during which we were called out of our respective classes and assembled in the office of the Lord High Executioner.

Mr. Gerstenblut had fifteen or twenty cards on his desk. "What do you fellows know about this?" he asked, handing cards to each of us.

"It's in French," Captain Colossal said.

"It has your name on it," I said.

"It says that you don't exist," Igor said.

"And what do you weirdos have to do with these?" Mr. Gerstenblut asked.

"I'm afraid we can't tell you," Venustiano Carranza (President of Mexico) said.

"And why not?"

"Because you don't exist."

Kevin Shapiro, Boy Orphan, Chapter Eleven Thousand Six Hundred.

So that was why it had been the easiest fight Kevin had ever been in. No wonder the new kid hadn't been able to land a single punch. "That's right, you miserable skunk," Mr. Jarvis said, "you beat up a blind boy." Kevin felt the hot tears well up in his eyes—his eyes that could see. Mr. Jarvis was right—he was a miserable skunk. How could he have been so stupid? What made it worse, Kevin sort of liked the new kid. He hadn't wanted to fight him. Something had caused Kevin to lose all control when the kid made that remark about homosexuals. Kevin wondered what had made him so mad. And he really liked the kid.

Mr. Gerstenblut told us that he was going to let us off because he didn't have any proof—but he was going to watch us. He said that we were nihilists, and he wasn't going to stand for any of that at Himmler.

We looked up nihilist in the library. We were tickled. Of course we weren't nihilists—Dadaists are constructive artists—but we all agreed, if we couldn't have been Dadaists, nihilism would have been a fairly decent second choice.

6

Imagine our surprise when we found out that there was a kid actually named Kevin Shapiro in the school! The Indiana Zephyr was the one to first discover this item of historically important information. The Wild Dada Ducks were all excited to think that there was an actual person bearing the name of the hero of our communal creation, *Kevin Shapiro, Boy Orphan.*

"Who is this kid?" Igor asked. "What does he look like?"

"We will adopt him," the Honorable Venustiano Carranza (President of Mexico) said. "Kevin Shapiro will be an orphan no more!"

"Yes," I said, "we should adopt this flesh-and-blood

Kevin Shapiro in honor of the hero of our Dada young-adult novel."

"But let's keep our interest in the fortunate young man a secret!" the Indiana Zephyr said.

"A dark secret," said Igor.

"Good! Good!" said the Honorable Venustiano Carranza (President of Mexico). "We will become the secret helpers of this Kevin Shapiro."

"We will help him to lead a full, rich, Dadaistic life!" I shouted.

"And he will never know who is helping him!" Captain Colossal said.

We were all getting very excited about the existence of a real-life Kevin Shapiro.

To tell the truth, we had all been getting fairly fed up with the Kevin Shapiro story we took turns telling, and I, for one, had the feeling that it might be time to kill him off once and for all. Now, the news that there was a real Kevin, and that he was going to be unknowingly adopted by the Wild Dada Ducks, breathed new life into our little artistic circle.

The only Wild Dada Duck who knew what the real Kevin Shapiro looked like was the Indiana Zephyr. We got up from the table where we had been discussing this remarkable development, and went for a little stroll around the lunchroom, so the Indiana Zephyr could point out our new adoptee.

It never fails to strike me, when the Wild Dada Ducks go anywhere, what a dignified and impressive picture we must make. Dressed in the finest Dada taste, serious, and intelligent looking, the Wild Dada Ducks are as fine a body of young men as anyone could hope to see.

We made our little promenade around the lunchroom, the Indiana Zephyr looking for our darling child, Kevin Shapiro. At last he pointed him out. "That's him over there," the Indiana Zephyr whispered.

Kevin Shapiro was better than any of us could have hoped. He was perfect. In fact, he was wonderful. He was magnificent. He was short, maybe five-two, and skinny. His hair was pale blond, and he wore it in a style known as a flattop. This is a crew cut with the hair standing up straight. The hair at the sides of the head is longer then the hair at the top of the head. The total effect is that of making one's head appear flat. It's a 1950s style that has come back into fashion because of some pre-Dada rock groups. Kevin Shapiro also had glasses, big cumbersome-looking plastic ones. His skin was very pale, and he had a little nose. We fell in love with him instantly.

Kevin Shapiro, never dreaming of his good fortune, was hunched over a box of Grape-Nuts, which he had opened by pulling apart the flaps on the side of the box, along the dotted lines. Into the waxed paper lining of the box, Kevin Shapiro had poured the contents of a carton of milk. The milk was dribbling out the corners of the box as he ate the cereal with a plastic spoon.

"This is auspicious," the Honorable Venustiano Carranza (President of Mexico) said to the rest of the Wild Dada Ducks. "Grape-Nuts is a Dada food, especially when you eat it out of the carton like that."

"Munch on, little Kevin Shapiro," Captain Colossal said, under his breath. "The Wild Dada Ducks will watch over you from this day forward."

7

"The first thing we ought to do," said the Honorable Venustiano Carranza (President of Mexico), "before we start helping Kevin Shapiro, is to find out all we can about the adorable little fellow."

This is the reason that the Honorable Venustiano Carranza (President of Mexico) is the undisputed leader of the Wild Dada Ducks. His foresight and methodical thinking is equalled only by his great artistic talent and Dadaistic style. It was agreed then and there, in the lunchroom, while Kevin Shapiro was finishing up his Grape-Nuts, that we would do exhaustive research about our little adopted boy.

Each of us, without being obvious or calling attention

to himself, would endeavor to find out all there was to find out about Kevin. In this way, the Honorable Venustiano Carranza (President of Mexico) pointed out, we would be able to see if there were any areas of deficiency in the life of our little adoptling. We would begin by supplying whatever Kevin lacked. Later we would help him to become a great culture hero—all without ever revealing ourselves, of course.

It was agreed that the following day, after school, we would meet at the Balkan Falcon Drug Company across the street from Himmler High, and discuss the information we had gathered.

The Balkan Falcon Drug Company is our favorite meeting place. It is generally shunned by other Himmler High students because of the foul temper of the fat old lady behind the counter, and the poor quality of the soda fountain—warm soda, filthy spoons, inedible hamburgers, and the like. However, the Wild Dada Ducks like the place, because it has booths, it's never crowded, and raisin toast costs only twenty cents an order.

So it was that the Wild Dada Ducks gathered at the Balkan Falcon Drug Company after school the following afternoon. Having been insulted by the fat old lady behind the counter, and having provided ourselves with raisin toast and hot chocolate in grimy cups, we proceeded to report to one another on what we had learned about our dear little Kevin Shapiro.

As each Wild Dada Duck spoke, I took notes. When everyone had made his report, I read back to the others all I had written:

26

Kevin Shapiro is a freshman. He is an average student, and likes Biology best of all his classes. His least favorite class is Physical Education, in which class his performance is perfectly miserable. He is nearsighted, and wears his glasses all the time. He lives in an apartment in one of the new buildings near Mesmer Park with his parents. He has no brothers or sisters. Kevin's family has a late-model Japanese sedan, a color television, and an old cocker spaniel, named Henry, who is overweight. Kevin walks Henry twice a day, before he leaves for school, and when he returns in the afternoon. In the evening Kevin's father walks Henry. Kevin has few friends. Those people he does know are mostly involved in comic book collecting. None of them go to Himmler. Kevin has a fairly large collection of old comic books, and almost every Saturday he goes around the city, looking for comics in various used-book stores. Every year, Kevin attends the comic collector's convention, where he buys, sells, and trades. His favorite comics are science-fiction ones. He also likes science-fiction movies.

All of this information had been assembled without any of the Wild Dada Ducks questioning Kevin directly, or drawing any special attention to themselves. We had found all this out by following Kevin, and by engaging various people in casual conversation—working in our questions about Kevin in such a subtle way that nobody ever suspected that we were interested in gathering information about him. Naturally, we were very proud of ourselves. We had gathered quite a lot of highly significant information about our beloved little friend, entirely in secret, and in the space of a little more than twenty-four hours.

"Now," said the Honorable Venustiano Carranza (President of Mexico), "let's discuss what all this data tells us about the lucky lad we have decided to guide and help without his knowledge."

"He leads the most boring life I ever heard of," Igor said.

"There isn't a trace of Dada consciousness in anything he does," Captain Colossal said.

"Except the fat cocker spaniel," I put in.

"Yes," said the Indiana Zephyr, "the fat cocker spaniel has some style, but it isn't really enough to make a Dadaist out of little Kevin, our adopted child."

"I agree," said the Honorable Venustiano Carranza (President of Mexico). "It's hard to tell where to begin helping Kevin Shapiro. The sad truth is, he's evidently a nerd."

"But there's hope," Igor said. "We might be able to rehabilitate him."

"Exactly!" said the Indiana Zephyr. "We have to do something to shake Kevin out of his dull, normal, un-Dada life-style."

"That will cost you forty cents," said the Honorable Venustiano Carranza (President of Mexico). "Pay each Wild Dada Duck ten cents for saying 'life-style.' "

There are fines for using certain words—such as life-style. If a Wild Dada Duck should say, "Have a nice day," it can cost him five dollars.

The Indiana Zephyr fished out four dimes, and

handed them around. "Well, you know what I mean," he said.

"Look out! Here comes you-know-who!" Igor said.

Kevin Shapiro had just entered the Balkan Falcon Drug Company. He walked toward the booth where we were sitting. We hadn't seen Kevin Shapiro walking before this. He had a fascinating walk. He sort of bobbed up and down, and worked his shoulders as he walked, as though he was listening to music—with a bad beat.

Kevin Shapiro came right up to our booth. He stopped walking, but continued to hunch his shoulders.

"Quit asking questions about me!" he said.

There was an uncomfortable moment of silence. Finally the Honorable Venustiano Carranza (President of Mexico) spoke. "You want us to quit doing what?" El Presidente asked, looking puzzled.

"Just quit!" Kevin Shapiro said.

"I assure you, old fellow," Captain Colossal said, "we have no idea what you're talking about."

"I'll punch out your face, see?" Kevin Shapiro said. He shook a pale skinny fist under the nose of Captain Colossal. "Just quit, that's all."

Kevin Shapiro turned, hunched his shoulders, and bobbed out of the Balkan Falcon Drug Company.

29

8

"He's a genius!" the Indiana Zephyr said.

"Definitely," Igor said.

"I think he's more than a genius," Captain Colossal said.

"I think he may be God," the Honorable Venustiano Carranza (President of Mexico) said.

"Definitely," I said.

It was clear to the Wild Dada Ducks that Kevin Shapiro had plenty of style, insolence, and punkishness —the raw materials of personal greatness. We loved and admired our adopted boy more than ever.

"We have to do something really wonderful for Kevin Shapiro," the Indiana Zephyr said.

"Yes," said the honorable Venustiano Carranza (President of Mexico), "nothing is too good for little Kevin. He will inspire our Dada masterpiece."

"But what are we going to do?" I asked.

"How about printing up cards again?" Captain Colossal asked. "They could say Kevin Shapiro is the greatest."

"That's not nearly big enough," said the Indiana Zephyr. "I don't mean to suggest that there's anything wrong with the idea of issuing a Dada card—the Horace Gerstenblut card was a great work of Art—but this is for Kevin. It has to be special."

We all agreed. The Wild Dada Ducks fell silent, chewing the crusts of our raisin toast, all of us trying to think up something magnificent enough to do for Kevin Shapiro.

"We want to call everybody's attention to the fact that Kevin Shapiro is a great person, isn't that right?" I asked.

"Yes," said Igor, "so what's your idea?"

"I don't have an idea yet," I said, "I just wanted to make sure I understood what we're after."

"A person as great as Kevin Shapiro ought to be world famous," El Presidente said.

"That's right!" Captain Colossal said.

"It would be wrong for only us Wild Dada Ducks to know about Kevin Shapiro," Igor said.

"We ought to let the whole world know what a splendid person Kevin Shapiro is," I said.

"Aren't there special guys who work for famous people—movie stars, and politicians, and people like that?" the Indiana Zephyr asked. "You know, they get their names in the paper, and they make sure everybody knows how great they are."

"That's right," I said, "publicity agents, they're called."

"That's it!" the Honorable Venustiano Carranza (President of Mexico) said. "That's what we have to do for little Kevin Shapiro! We have to make him famous and loved by everybody!"

"We'll be his publicity agents!"

"We'll get everybody to appreciate him!"

"We'll make him famous!"

"This is a chance to do something not only for our beloved Kevin Shapiro, but for the whole world!"

"This is a great day for world Dada Culture!"

"So what do we do first?"

"How about printing up a lot of cards?"

"Captain Colossal, can't you think of anything but printing up cards?" the Honorable Venustiano Carranza (President of Mexico) asked.

"Maybe we could print up posters," I said.

"That's it!" everybody said. "A really great poster of Kevin Shapiro—in color."

"We'll print thousands!"

"Everybody will want them!"

"It's perfect!"

"Wait a second!" Igor said. "That will cost a lot of money—probably hundreds. Do we have that much?"

The fact was, the Wild Dada Ducks didn't have any money to speak of. Between us we hardly had hundreds of cents, let alone dollars.

"Isn't that always the way?" the Honorable Venus-tiano Carranza (President of Mexico) said. "Lack of money once again thwarts a great Artistic enterprise. We'll have to keep thinking."

We kept thinking.

The more we thought, the more the idea of printing up something in the school print shop seemed to have merit. First of all, it didn't cost anything. Captain Colossal could run off the cards almost any day after school, and as long as we were willing to use whatever scrap paper the print shop had lying around, the whole production would be free.

The Honorable Venustiano Carranza (President of Mexico) grumbled quite a bit about printing cards again. He wanted to do something we had never done before. However, since no one including El Presidente could come up with anything that was both good and possible, we finally fell back on Captain Colossal and the printing press. The Honorable Venustiano Carranza (President of Mexico) insisted that we at least make these cards a bit larger than the last batch, and try our best to give them a decent Dada quality. We spent the next hour working on the text for the card. When we finished, and everybody had expressed approval, we gave the final copy to Captain Colossal, with instructions to do his utmost to give the thing an appearance we could all be proud of.

Two days later, in the Balkan Falcon Drug Company, Captain Colossal presented an edition of two thousand cards. They were excellent. Not only was the printing job superior, but the Captain had managed to get some very handsome green cardboard, and some printer's cuts showing pictures of this and that which he had artistically arranged to make the cards even more impressive. The whole effect was very fine, and we were all pleased.

KEVIN SHAPIRO
is the
GREATEST Human
Humanoid
Bioelectronic entity
Funky Dude
& Disco Dancer
OF ALL TIME

9

It is funny how fate takes its cut. That is one of the favorite sayings of the Wild Dada Ducks. It means that however carefully you plan things, however much you're sure how things are supposed to turn out—something you never thought of can change everything. Fate will take its cut.

When the Wild Dada Ducks planned and executed the handsome works of Art in honor of Kevin Shapiro, events were already moving in a direction none of us could have guessed. But that is always the way things work. That is why Dada is the greatest Art movement. The Dadaist assumes things are going to go wrong—or at least in an unpredictable direction—so he isn't surprised when it happens. He is surprised when it doesn't.

We distributed the Kevin Shapiro cards in the same manner as the Horace Gerstenblut cards. That is, we left stacks of them in all the bathrooms. Once again we had cause to wish there were some girls in the Duckettes, as darting in and out of the girls' bathrooms was dangerous and scary. However, we got the cards distributed without anyone seeing us, and without meeting anyone apt to get upset.

Because the Wild Dada Ducks are constantly preoccupied with Dada Art and Philosophy, we frequently neglect the events of day-to-day life at Himmler High School. Ask any of us who won the big basketball game last night—and we will ask who was playing. It isn't that we necessarily disapprove of such activities—it's just that you can't lead the way in an Artistic revolution and keep track of every little detail.

So it happened that none of us had the slightest idea that the day we distributed our sincere tribute to Kevin Shapiro was also the day of the Himmler High School Student Council election.

Just as they had done with the Horace Gerstenblut cards, our fellow students picked up the new Kevin Shapiro edition, talked about it, passed cards around to their friends, and tried to guess who Kevin Shapiro might be, and what the cards meant. Of course, that is not the proper way to appreciate the cards. They are works of Art to be enjoyed, and experienced—not analyzed. However, that is not our concern. As Dada Artists, we provide the Art, the public can do what it likes with it. Besides, the message of the cards was perfectly obvious. The cards were intended to notify the world in general, and Himmler High in particular, that Kevin Shapiro was an exceptionally great human being.

In fact, that part of our message did appear to have been picked up by a great many people, because, after having a look at the cards, discussing them, and swapping them around, ninety-seven percent of the students at Himmler High went and voted for Kevin Shapiro.

They voted for him for Student Council President, and for all the positions on the student council. All told, Kevin Shapiro received about 28,000 votes from approximately 4,000 students.

We didn't know anything about this, because the voting was by secret ballot. The results of the election would be announced in an assembly of the whole school the next day.

The day of the Student Council election was like any other day in the lives of the Wild Dada Ducks. We had executed our Artwork, we went to our classes, we picked up ballots for the student council election, and each voted for Kevin Shapiro for all seven places, including Student Council President.

At the assembly the following day, the official candidates for office were all lined up, sitting in a row on folding chairs on the auditorium stage. They were wearing suits and dresses. They had sat in the same order, wearing the same outfits, the week before when each candidate had made a campaign speech.

Mr. Gerstenblut, the vice-principal, and Mr. Winter,

the principal, were both on stage too. Mr. Winter made a short speech about how we were lucky to live in a democracy and be able to vote in elections, and the usual stuff they tell you at school elections. The Wild Dada Ducks have nothing against democracy, except that it doesn't go nearly far enough—but the thing about being elected to a school office that we find boring is that you wouldn't get to pass any real laws, even if you got elected.

Miss Steele, the chairman of the election committee, came out to read the results of the tabulation of all the votes.

"We have a very remarkable situation here," Miss Steele said. "It seems there have been a great many write-in votes for a candidate who hadn't even announced that he was in the race. Now ordinarily, the election committee would insist on the rule that states that if a candidate for Student Council President is not one of those duly nominated, votes for that person will be discounted. The rule further states that if the person with the winning number of votes is not one of those duly nominated, the duly nominated person with the next largest number of votes will be elected. However, in this election, one extremely popular young man has gotten practically all of the votes, for all the offices on the Student Council—and, as you may have guessed, he is not one of those duly nominated."

"The committee feels that it will be best if we declare the election as having miscarried," Miss Steele went on to considerable booing. "We are going to hold another election, by show of hands, here this morning—but in

38

the interest of fairness, we would like to invite the young man who got so many votes to come up on the stage and say a few words. You've already heard from the other fine candidates. Now, will the young man who has already demonstrated that he has the confidence of his fellow students, please approach the stage? Will Kevin Shapiro please come up and say a few words?"

There was a thunderous outburst of applause. There was also a good deal of neck-craning and looking around, since almost nobody in the school knew who Kevin Shapiro was.

From the very last row in the auditorium a small thin figure shuffled and bobbed down the aisle, and then bounded up the steps to the stage. It was our boy. It was Kevin Shapiro. The Wild Dada Ducks started a cheer that was wildly taken up by everyone else in the school. Kevin Shapiro, cool as you please, stood on the stage, waiting for the cheering and clapping to die down. I noticed for the first time that Kevin had these really klutzy shoes. They looked like Frankenstein boots. I think he picked shoes with the thickest possible soles, in an attempt to get an extra inch of height. The shoes made Kevin Shapiro look incredibly Dada. He shifted from foot to foot and waited for the crowd to be quiet.

Finally the last whistle and foot-stomp and cheer had echoed through the auditorium and Kevin Shapiro spoke.

"Hey," he said, "I don't want to be any slob President of the Student Council. Don't vote for me, see?

ote for these idiots here."

The applause was deafening. It went on for about ten minutes.

Kevin was re-elected by a landslide.

10

The Wild Dada Ducks were filled with pride and delight. In just one short day following our public expression of appreciation, Kevin Shapiro had been almost unanimously recognized as the finest example of humanity in the whole school. The crowd in the auditorium was going crazy. The cheering had consolidated into a continuous roar, as Kevin Shapiro, now elected for the second time—this time by acclamation—approached the microphone.

It took a long time for the audience to become quiet. Kevin Shapiro, who appeared to us to be a born public speaker and leader of men, patiently waited until the last expression of enthusiasm had been uttered. He held up both hands in a gesture for silence, which was at the same time friendly, endearing. Kevin Shapiro was the most beloved person in all of Himmler High School at that moment.

"Look," he began, "I thought I made myself clear. I do not want to be on your stupid Student Council. Just leave me alone. Anybody bothers me, I'll bash his face in, see?" Kevin shook a fist meaningfully, and returned to his seat.

There was another spontaneous demonstration of support for Kevin Shapiro, but no amount of cheering and chanting could induce him to leave his auditorium seat and speak to the students again. The crowd showed no sign of leaving peaceably, and finally Mr. Winter, who has an astonishingly loud voice, took over.

Mr. Winter declared the day's exercises over, and by executive order abolished all elections in the school until further notice.

This is why the Wild Dada Ducks—and apparently Kevin Shapiro—do not take school elections seriously. Mr. Winter has the last word.

The crowd left the auditorium in an ugly mood. Every teacher in Himmler High knew that the rest of the day was going to be grim. There was a lot of resentment expressed toward Mr. Winter for abolishing elections, and this resentment extended to all figures of authority, especially teachers.

Somehow, nobody seemed to be angry at little Kevin Shapiro. He had twice rejected the nearly unanimous vote of the entire student body—and in no uncertain

42

terms. He had called them stupid, and made it plain that he couldn't be bothered to serve as Student Council president. And yet, no one appeared to have taken offense. The students of Himmler High School respected Kevin's wish, and mostly left him alone. It was really unheard-of behavior. I mean, the majority of the students are far from being philosophers, let alone Dadaists. To tell the truth, most of the kids are only human on a technicality. They take great mindless pride in their school—they go to all the games and scream bloody murder—about once every other year there is a mass fist-fight with the students from Kissinger High School, our great rival.

Now, Kevin Shapiro, a little, skinny, bespectacled kid, had openly rejected one of the institutions of Himmler High. In effect he had rejected the whole population of the school—and nobody tried to kill him! The only thing the Wild Dada Ducks could make of this remarkable behavior was that, like us, simply anybody who saw Kevin Shapiro could not help loving him. Captain Colossal said he had charisma. Igor said it was star quality. Whatever it was, Kevin definitely had it, and we were all very proud of him. We were ashamed to remember that up until the last minute, we were all going to vote for the Marquis de Sade.

11

Of course, school elections, and assemblies, and all of those things are dumb. Anyone would realize it, if it were given any thought—but generally, nobody thinks about those things. The Wild Dada Ducks do not approve of school elections, naturally, because we are for the abolishment of government as we know it. We want the machines to take over. That is, we want ordinary, loyal, everyday machines, like dishwashers and buses and pencil sharpeners, to take over the government—not computers and robots, which are probably really in charge already. The Wild Dada Ducks do not approve of school elections, but the ordinary unenlightened Himmler High School students just love them.

At least that's what we thought until the election of Kevin Shapiro (who refused to serve). To tell the truth, we weren't sure what was going through the minds of our fellow students. Mostly, we were proud of how popular our boy, Kevin Shapiro, had become because of the distribution of our Dada card. We didn't consider what might be the innermost thoughts of the other kids in the school.

Later we got an idea of what the whole school thought of Kevin Shapiro.

They worshipped him.

Kevin was the single biggest hero in the school. He was the only hero in the school. In a single moment, he had expressed the secret truth about school elections, the school, the world, being a kid—everything. Every kid in the auditorium that day realized the reality of his situation when Kevin Shapiro said that he didn't want to be on any stupid student council. Most kids wouldn't have said anything like that, even if they were thinking it—but Kevin did.

Like the Wild Dada Ducks, every kid in the school had realized that Kevin Shapiro had a style all his own. Just as we had predicted, he was a natural leader.

Kevin's wish that he be left alone only made everybody love and respect him more. All the girls were in love with him. All the boys were afraid of him. Simply anybody would have died of happiness if Kevin Shapiro had smiled at them, or winked, or spoken, or anything.

All this was true, but nobody actually realized it—or realized the extent or importance of it. When we filed out of the auditorium that day, nobody was conscious of the great event that had taken place—with the possible exception of Mr. Winter and Mr. Gerstenblut, both of whom looked worried. They had taken courses in being a principal, and they knew they had the makings of an uprising on their hands. They knew this, or they may have known it—but there was nothing they could do but wait.

The Wild Dada Ducks were not worried, even when Kevin Shapiro passed by us in the crush of people leaving the auditorium. He smiled a grim smile, and rubbed his belly, as if he was thinking about something good to eat. "I'll get you for this," he said.

We just attributed his remark and gesture to his natural charm, and were even a little flattered that he had spoken to us. We didn't understand that Kevin Shapiro was the king of the school—and we didn't understand the power a king has.

Everything appeared to go back to normal at once. As far as the Wild Dada Ducks were concerned, the election and the assembly in the auditorium were part of the Dada Work we had started with the cards—and it had been our most successful exercise so far. Now it was over, and we all felt good about it.

12

Nothing changed at first. The day after the student council elections, and the day after that, life at Himmler High School was normal, average. Students went from class to class, the Wild Dada Ducks met to discuss Art and Culture in the Balkan Falcon Drug Company, and Kevin Shapiro ate alone in the lunchroom. Mr. Winter and Mr. Gerstenblut appeared in the halls very often, looking alert and nervous, as though they expected to find something important going on—but nothing was going on.

That's what they thought.

That's what we thought.

That's what everyone thought.

It was on the third day after the election that the Fanatical Praetorians first appeared. We didn't know they were the Fanatical Praetorians at first. They were all the kids in Himmler High who were shorter than Kevin Shapiro, and they all had sailor hats.

These sailor hats were of the variety worn by Donald Duck in the early cartoons. They were soft and white, with a ribbon hanging down in the back. I don't know where they got them. There was a blue band around the bottom of the hats with the words *S.S. Popnick,* printed in white. They must have been Navy surplus, but from which country's navy, I don't know.

The short kids in sailor/duck hats all sat in the lunch-room, not too close to Kevin Shapiro, but surrounding him on all sides. They all ate Grape-Nuts from little cartons into which they had poured milk. Most of them had big Frankenstein shoes like Kevin Shapiro. All of them had sworn an oath to protect Kevin with their lives.

Kevin Shapiro had recruited the Fanatical Praetorians, and administered the oath. Not only had he organized a bodyguard, and, as we gradually learned—an illegal government within the school—Kevin Shapiro had also started an Art Movement.

It was called Heroic Realism.

We didn't find all these things out at once. At first, all we knew was that a bunch of little kids in sailor hats were trailing around, a respectful distance behind Kevin Shapiro, and if anyone approached him or tried to talk to him, they would make a wall of their bodies, and threaten the person who intended to approach.

Since Kevin Shapiro didn't like to talk to people, and mostly wanted to be left alone, there weren't many confrontations with the Fanatical Praetorians. It seemed a little weird, and that was all.

Then came Heroic Realism. As we had found out when we were doing research about him, Kevin Shapiro was a big comic book fan. It turned out that what he liked best about comic books was the artwork. The Wild Dada Ducks had declared comic books unartistic a long time ago. Not only did we find the stories predictable and boring, but the pictures seemed particularly awful to us. For the most part, they showed guys with too many muscles and heads too small for their bodies.

Kevin Shapiro loved comic books.

Heroic Realism declared that anything that wasn't a comic book was no good. Anybody who didn't like comic books was no good. Conversely, anybody who liked comic books was a great person. That, as far as we could make out, was all there was to Heroic Realism.

Every student in Himmler High was a Heroic Realist. Except us, of course. Also, every student in Himmler High recognized Kevin Shapiro as his supreme leader.

Kevin Shapiro was a good deal more than president of the student council. It was obvious why he had scorned that basically meaningless honor. Kevin Shapiro had become undisputed king of Himmler High. His word was law. Of course, he practically never said anything, but if he had said anything it would have been law.

Obviously he communicated to the Fanatical Praetorians. If Kevin Shapiro wanted to tell anybody anything, it was done through the Fanatical Praetorians. For example, if you were sitting in the lunchroom, a half-dozen Fanatical Praetorians might come over to you and say, "Kevin doesn't want you sitting there." So you'd move. Everybody was afraid of the Fanatical Praetorians.

They were little, but there were a lot of them. Also, they had learned to imitate Kevin's special way of being persuasive. "Look," they'd say, "we'll punch out your face, see?" It never failed to get results.

Big kids, who had formerly been known as bullies, cowered and cringed before the short kids in the Donald Duck hats. Some kids wanted to become Fanatical Praetorians, but they weren't short enough.

After school every day Kevin Shapiro would be escorted away from the school by a big crowd of Fanatical Praetorians. They even guarded him on weekends. Once I saw him leafing through comic books in a store downtown, while ten or eleven shrimps in sailor hats stood around him.

After a week or two, everybody was sufficiently afraid of the Fanatical Praetorians that they were obeyed even when they were alone. Even the teachers learned to respect them. In the Biology class taken by the Indiana Zephyr and Captain Colossal, there was only one Fanatical Praetorian, a kid named Shep Stoneman. It seems Shep Stoneman got into an argument with the teacher. The teacher wanted Shep to remove his sailor hat. Shep didn't want to. Finally, Shep told the entire class to get up and leave the room. They did it.

Mr. Winter and Mr. Gerstenblut were all over the building, dealing with problems caused by the Fanatical Praetorians. There were a great many comic books being circulated in the school because of the Heroic Realism movement, and there had been a number of tense moments between teachers and Fanatical Praetorians.

At one point, Mr. Winter outlawed the wearing of hats in school. The next day, by order of the Fanatical Praetorians, every kid in the school wore a hat of some kind all day, and a general strike was threatened. That is, all the kids wore hats except the Wild Dada Ducks.

This constituted a moral dilemma for us. Here was the breakdown of the normal un-Dada order, which we had all wished for, but we found we couldn't go along with the hats-on order which emanated from Kevin Shapiro—a hero we ourselves had created. We didn't exactly know why we felt we could not go along with it. There was something about Heroic Realism that made it impossible—but it was more than that. We had been nonconformists for so long that it just didn't feel right to go along with everyone else—and there was something else too, but we couldn't say what it was.

Of course, the hat-wearing was a complete success. What could Mr. Winter do? He couldn't very well call in the police. Nobody was doing anything destructive —they were wearing hats, that was all. He couldn't suspend everybody. He couldn't very well write to everyone's parents, and say that little Johnny had worn a hat on such-and-such a day and was therefore suspended. It was a clear victory for Kevin and his loyal followers. That was everybody but the Wild Dada Ducks.

Mr. Winter wriggled out of his defeat, ungracefully, by having all the homeroom teachers read something about how styles change, and how Himmler High students have always been models of good grooming and acceptable dress, and that if hats were "in" then the administration of the school wasn't about to spoil anybody's fun, and how Mr. Winter always kept up with the times, and had even personally been to a disco with his wife, and sometimes didn't wear a necktie.

It didn't fool anybody. The Fanatical Praetorians were running the place, and they obeyed nobody but Kevin Shapiro. It only remained to see what Kevin would decide to do next.

13

The Wild Dada Ducks were especially interested in what Kevin Shapiro would do next. Obviously, it had not gone unnoticed that we had been the only ones not to wear hats during the protest. The truth was, we were somewhat afraid of what the Fanatical Praetorians might do to us. One thing was certain, they would not do anything except on Kevin Shapiro's order.

The next thing Kevin Shapiro got interested in was making sure that everybody in the school ate Grape-Nuts. This project interested him so much that he actually spoke to the assembled kids in the lunchroom one day.

Kevin got up, and struck a pose indicating that he

was about to speak. Even without the shushing and fingers to lips of the Fanatical Praetorians, the room would have fallen silent in a hurry. This was to be the first public utterance of Kevin Shapiro since he had turned down the student council.

"Grape-Nuts is good!" he said.

After that no lunch at Himmler High School did not include a little carton of Grape-Nuts cereal with milk poured into the waxed paper liner. The school lunchroom didn't have enough in stock at first, and kids brought Grape-Nuts from home. Lunchtime became a symphony of crunching and slurping.

Fearing for our lives, and arguing that as Dadaists we had already approved of Grape-Nuts, the Wild Dada Ducks joined in the cereal eating. Secretly, we hoped that our failure to wear hats that day when everybody else wore them might be forgotten, especially since we were eating Grape-Nuts like the Heroic Realists.

And, in fact, in seemed that our act of disloyalty had been forgotten. In the days that followed, nothing special happened. Of course, the fulminations of the Heroic Realists annoyed us no end. Kids went on and on about the beauty of comic books, and our Dada sensibilities were continually offended by snatches of overheard conversation about Mouse-Man and Wonder Wombat—but in general, life was bearable at Himmler High School.

Kevin Shapiro's main concern seemed to be the continued eating of Grape-Nuts. Often at lunchtime, he could be seen contentedly surveying the spectacle of a great many kids, all working away at their little boxes of cereal.

The lunchroom at Himmler High is large, as is the school itself. While the room is not capable of containing the whole student population, a good thousand can eat there at once. Nowadays, they ate a good thousand boxes of Grape-Nuts at once.

Kevin Shapiro's concern about the cereal eating was such that he actually spoke again. This time he climbed up onto a table, and gestured for silence.

"Get 'em good and soggy," he said.

After this, people took considerably longer with their lunches. Under the ever-watchful eye of Kevin and his bodyguard, it became customary to let the milk and cereal sit uneaten for ten or fifteen minutes, the Grape-Nuts absorbing all the milk that did not run out the corners of the carton.

One day, a deputation of Fanatical Praetorians actually walked around the lunchroom, inspecting people's Grape-Nuts to see that they were good and soggy.

A couple of days after the Praetorian tour of inspection, Kevin Shapiro once again, and for the last time, addressed the assembled lunching students.

Again he stood upon a table, not too far from where the Wild Dada Ducks were sitting. He had his carton of well-sogged Grape-Nuts in his hand.

"Look!" said Kevin Shapiro. "Watch me!"

Kevin Shapiro turned the box over, and dumped the soggy contents into his cupped right hand.

"Down with Dada!" he shouted and hurled the

mess of dripping Grape-Nuts right into the face of the Honorable Venustiano Carranza (President of Mexico).

What followed was horrible. The Wild Dada Ducks were served at least one thousand portions of Grape-Nuts. They were thrown at us, poured over our heads, stuffed down our pants, and mushed into our hair. The massacre took place so quickly that we never had time to get out of our chairs. We sat there, stunned, and were turned into living, dripping statues.

When we left the lunchroom we squished as we walked, and left a sloppy trail of cereal.

14

Not long after the Grape-Nuts devastation, it seems Kevin Shapiro disbanded the invincible Fanatical Praetorians. Heroic Realism appeared to wane as an Art Movement, and conditions at the school returned entirely to normal.

Kevin Shapiro, refusing to do anything to exploit the total power he had over his fellow students, was gradually forgotten, and could be seen hunched over his Grape-Nuts at lunch, alone as before.

Whenever he saw any of the Wild Dada Ducks he laughed to himself.

The Wild Dada Ducks left him alone.

We also suspended our program of cultural improvement for our fellow students. We continued to meet after school every day in the Balkan Falcon Drug Company. There we pursued our discussions of Art and Philosophy.

For about a week we made no mention of our experience in the lunchroom with the Grape-Nuts. Finally, it seemed time to discuss its implications and historical importance.

"Does it seem possible," asked Igor, "that Kevin Shapiro seized control of the entire school, just so he could have us covered with wet breakfast cereal?"

No one was sure. It could have been planned from the start, or it could have just been an idea that occured to him at the moment.

"The important question," said Captain Colossal, "is what is the significance of Kevin's rise to power, and the Grape-Nuts attack? What does it mean in philosophical terms?"

"Yes," said the Indiana Zephyr, "what is the moral of the story?"

"It has no moral," said the Honorable Venustiano Carranza (President of Mexico), "it is a Dada story."

end